THIS BOOK BELONGS TO

SHADOW

Lucy Christopher
Anastasia Suvorova

LANTANA PUBLISHING

In our old house, Ma told me
there was nothing to be scared of.
No monsters hiding behind doors,
or in wardrobes, or under beds.

She said there were no dark
places at all.

But in the new house, under my new bed,
THAT's where I found Shadow.

We both just lay still.

Here were cobwebs that hadn't been swept for years. Dust piles big as rats.

Shadow hid among it all.

I told Ma about Shadow, but she couldn't see. She thought I was making him up.

So I crawled in with him. I reached for him in the dark and he didn't go away.

One day, Shadow came out. We played hide and seek in the new room that was mine now. He was a king and I his queen.

At night, our scarves knitted together. In the dark, Shadow and me were the same.

I didn't go to school and neither did Shadow. We slid down the banisters and drew on the walls.

We found the attic. Together we danced across the couch, and hid in the packing boxes.

But still, Ma couldn't see.

Sometimes Ma couldn't see for days.

One day, Shadow and me left. We crossed the road, passed the shop, and went into the forest.

The trees were huge and stretched to the sky. They made more shadows.

I tried to follow Shadow
but he was playing hide
and seek with the others.
I heard him laugh as he
slipped between the trees.

And then it was too dark.
There were no shadows left.

I cried that night in the forest,
but no one came.

I was all alone.

But after a while, a very long while, when I had no more tears to cry, there was the smallest crack of light.

And with it came a sound. I listened. It was just one word. My name. Again and again. Louder and louder.

I followed it like a thread.

I twisted between the roots of the huge swaying trees, finding my way back.

And there, in the middle of the forest, Ma was looking for me.

I sat beside her, and held her hand. Now I saw her shadow too. And she saw mine.

As the trees got thinner, it got easier to see.

We went out of the forest. Ma and me, together.

I tied my scarf to a branch for Shadow. So he wouldn't forget me, and so I could find him again if I needed to.

Ma and me passed the shop and crossed the road. We went back to the new house that was ours now.

I showed Ma all the best hiding
places. I always found her.
And she always found me.

We played all day.

Sometimes others joined in too.

We played until Ma and me
knew all the dark places in
our new house.

And we weren't scared.

Andy for the joy, Johanna for the light, and Emily for the spark: thank you.
Lucy

For Ma, who was always worried about losing me.
Anastasia

First published in the United Kingdom in 2019 by Lantana Publishing Ltd., London.
www.lantanapublishing.com

American edition published in 2019 by Lantana Publishing Ltd., UK.
info@lantanapublishing.com

Text © Lucy Christopher 2019
Illustration © Anastasia Suvorova 2019

The moral rights of the author and illustrator have been asserted.

Distributed in the United States and Canada by Lerner Publishing Group, Inc.
241 First Avenue North, Minneapolis, MN 55401 U.S.A.
For reading levels and more information, look for this title at www.lernerbooks.com
Cataloging-in-Publication Data Available.

Printed and bound in Europe.
Original artwork created digitally.

ISBN: 978-1-911373-83-4
eBook ISBN: 978-1-911373-86-5